Little
Peter's Railway
Grandpa Goes Bananas

by
Christopher Vine

The watercolour illustrations are by John Wardle

Published by
Christopher Vine 2016

Printed by The Amadeus Press
Copyright © 2016 Christopher Vine

ISBN 978-1-9088970-60

The Peter's Railway Series

Some transport museums are wonderful places; full of life and working exhibits. There are huge locomotives running outside or small models in glass cases which work when you press a button.

Please do not think that this story is about any of the preserved steam railways or the National Railway Museum in York. They all make huge efforts to keep old steam engines working so people can still be enchanted by them.

No, this is a story about another museum where nothing works. It is just a building full of dead, old machines. But not for long...

(To see that this story is possible, search the Internet for the film *A Great Railroad at Work 1942* – about 21 minutes into the film. Do not try to act out this story at home, or in a museum!)

Grandpa Goes Bananas

After several years of enjoying building their railway across the farm, Grandpa and Peter had decided to write everything down. The result was a famous series of books, all about their adventures, experiments and disasters!

One weekend, they were invited to an event at a transport museum to show their books to the public. They had also taken their engine, Fiery Fox, to demonstrate how a steam locomotive works.

Fiery Fox was on a display stand with a good fire in the boiler and plenty of steam. Grandpa had jacked up its driving wheels, above the track, so they could turn slowly. Kitty was blowing the whistle while Harry put coal on the fire and Peter explained to everyone how the engine worked.

During the day, they had all been admiring the huge but silent locomotive which was sitting right behind them on some short rails.

"It's such a shame," said Peter, after all the visitors had gone home, "that such a beautiful and awesome machine just sits there doing nothing. It's a bit like a dead animal in a glass case; it doesn't give you any idea of what it was really like."

The others agreed with him. It would be much better if they could see it working!

Grandpa explained that the museum had spent all of its money on their fantastic new building. They had nothing left to get the old machines working, so everything was still and quiet.

"But," he said with a glint in his eye, "I know a lot about that engine, and I've got an idea..."

"Would you like to bring an old steam locomotive back to life, just for one day?" Grandpa asked the children. "Yes please!" they all agreed.

"That engine," he explained, "was in perfect working order when she arrived at this museum. Even her boiler is in good condition. We could light the fire, raise steam and blow the whistle."

"We could even have the wheels going round and round, just like we did with Fiery Fox," Grandpa continued, getting really excited with his idea.

"But how can the wheels turn?" asked Peter.

"By oiling the driving wheels and the track," explained Grandpa, "to make it so slippery that the wheels can spin round without the engine moving. It was a trick they used to do in the old days, if they wanted to test an engine at the repair works."

Testing a locomotive
in the old days.

As an extra-special treat, Grandpa had arranged that they could spend the night in the museum, sleeping in an old carriage.

The building was now closed but they were all much too excited to go to bed. So, in the sleeping, dimly lit museum, the children got to work.

"The first thing to do," explained Grandpa, "is to fill the boiler with water. We can use the fire hose, but it will still take two or three hours."

Kitty and Harry pulled the long pipe up to the top of the boiler, while Peter and Grandpa opened a plug so they could poke the end inside.

"Turn it on!" Peter called down to Kitty. Seconds later, a rushing, gurgling sound told them the boiler was filling up.

While the boiler was filling with water, they started to get ready for lighting the fire.

"There's plenty of coal in the tender," observed Peter, "but we're going to need lots of small bits of wood to get the fire started."

"I know where there's plenty of wood," shouted Harry. "There's a whole load of broken wooden pallets, just beside the museum storage area. They would burn really well."

While Harry fetched armfuls of kindling wood, Peter and Kitty lifted it up into the engine's cab and stacked it in the firebox, ready for lighting.

Grandpa, meanwhile, had found a very old wood saw; it was one of the exhibits in the museum! He was using it to cut some wood into wedge-shaped blocks, to stop some of the wheels from moving.

At last the water gauges showed that the boiler was full enough. Now the fun could really start.

Grandpa had put an oil-soaked rag on the coal shovel and, being a farmer, he had a box of matches in his pocket. But of course, Peter, Harry and Kitty all wanted to be the one to light the fire.

"There's only one way to settle it," smiled Grandpa. "Eeny meeny miny moe..." he started. "Who wants to make it go?" It was Kitty who won.

"Great!" she grinned, striking a match and holding it to the oily rag (which was, in fact, Grandpa's handkerchief!). It lit instantly and Peter dropped it into the firebox and, using the shovel, pushed the burning hanky under some of the wood.

The dry wood caught quickly, and the flames lit up the children's faces with a lovely warm glow.

Every few minutes, Peter put a few shovelfuls of coal into the firebox. Slowly the fire burned hotter and hotter. The boiler began to sing quietly and little creaking, pinging sounds told the children that the old locomotive was coming back to life.

There was still lots to do. Grandpa put on the hand brake and put his wedges in front of some of the wheels. They didn't want the engine to take off through the wall of the museum!

Harry put oil in all of the little oil-cups and then put lots of oil on the track and all around the wheels, so they could slip round easily.

Kitty was up on the tender, filling it with more water for the boiler.

There was just one small problem. The museum was rapidly filling up with smoke!

Everyone had been so busy that they simply hadn't noticed the time. It was now morning and people were queuing outside, waiting to come into the museum.

"Whatever is going on?" asked one boy, pointing to smoke rising from vents on the roof.

"Looks like the museum's on fire!" shouted someone else. "Quick! Call the Fire Brigade!"

Just then, the front doors slid open and Grandpa appeared from inside. "Don't panic!" he called out calmly. "Everything's under control."

"We've put on a special show. Come on in and see a gigantic steam locomotive – working!"

Everyone ran into the museum, wondering what on earth they were going to see.

Entering the main hall, the sight that met their eyes was something they would never forget.

The old locomotive was now alive! There was smoke and sparks belching out of its chimney. The wheels were spinning round and round in a blur of motion, and the whole building was shaking. The noise, smell and heat were indescribable.

It was fantastic, magnificent. Monumental!

Peter was leaning out of the cab window and Kitty was blowing the whistle. All the while, Harry was furiously oiling the wheels and track so the monster engine didn't suddenly get a grip on the rails and shoot off through the wall of the museum.

The visitors stared, spellbound. They loved it. This is what a museum *should* be like!

Meanwhile, outside the museum things were getting quite exciting too.

Three fire engines, an ambulance and two police cars arrived with sirens wailing. They skidded to a halt at exactly the same time as the manager of the museum was arriving in his car!

Mr Jones leapt out and ran into his museum, with the firemen and policemen in hot pursuit.

"Whatever is going on?" he shouted above the noise. "You can't do that in my museum!"

Grandpa, realising that things had got a bit out of hand, stepped forward to try to calm him down. "We were just trying to show the visitors," he started to explain, "what a steam engine really looks like, when it's working..."

Unfortunately, this didn't seem to calm the manager down at all. In fact it seemed to make him even more angry. "You!" he shouted, pointing his finger at Grandpa. "In my office. Now!"

"You might have set the museum on fire," he roared, still jabbing his finger angrily. "You are in a whole load of trouble! and I'm going to..."

Just then, the telephone rang and Mr Jones snatched it up. "Yes?" he yelled. "Who are you?... The BBC?... You want to do what?..."

"It's the TV news crew," he hissed at Grandpa. "They've just arrived to film the disaster that you have caused. It's going to look terrible."

"You had better go and explain it yourself. You caused this mess, so you can take the blame!"

Poor Grandpa. He was very upset.

Back in the hall, they found the children talking to the TV cameras, and all the visitors were saying what a brilliant and exciting event it was.

"I'm very sorry I was so angry," said Mr Jones to Grandpa after a few minutes. "But it's clear that everyone loves what you have done. Thank you!"

"We've enjoyed it too!" chuckled Grandpa, very relieved. Then he settled down to watch his grandchildren playing trains – on an epic scale.

"Just don't forget to keep oiling those wheels!" he called out to Harry.

"Why?" asked Mr Jones. "Is that important?"

"I think it's probably best," replied Grandpa smiling, "if you don't know about that..."

The End.

Why Peter's Railway?

Since a very small boy, Chris has always loved everything mechanical, especially steam engines. The first workshop was in his bedroom where he made an electric go-kart when only 8, followed by a mini-bike powered by the engine from a petrol lawn mower.

He spent many holidays on a friend's farm where there was a miniature railway across a field, and so started a love of making model steam locomotives. The latest is Bongo, 8 feet long and the inspiration for Fiery Fox in the books.

Chris wanted to share his love and knowledge of railways and engineering: Peter's Railway is the result.

Books for children who love trains and engineering

Story   **Technical**   **History**   **Adventure**

The hardback books

The five hardback books tell the charming story of Peter and his Grandpa building and running their steam railway across the farm. At the ends of chapters are special how-it-works pages with simple (but accurate) explanations of what has been happening in the story. In addition, Grandpa tells some wonderful stories from the old days on the railways. Age range 6 - 12 years approx.

A new steam railway is born.

Points, turntables and Peter drives Fiery Fox.

The line is extended and The Great Railway Race.

They build a watermill to power the farm.

Peter helps save the world and makes lots of money!

Activity book with puzzles and colouring - paperback.

Hardback, 96 pages 17 x 24 cm with 30 watercolour pictures by John Wardle and 14 pages of clearly explained technical drawings. £11.99

Paperback books

A series of Peter's Railway in a smaller format. While the original books each contain several story or adventure threads, separate technical pages and Grandpa's tales, the small books concentrate on one aspect; an adventure, a tale from the old railways or a technical book. The four *Little* books are for younger readers.

An adventure on a Scottish holiday which ends with a bang!
Age 6 to 12 years

A true story about an unlucky engine and a brave fireman.
Age 6 to 12 years

A crazy mistake leads to disaster. One of Grandpa's true stories.
Age 6 to 12 years

A cab-ride in a modern diesel and a story from the old days.
Age 6 to 12 years

Our two heroes build a new locomotive from scrap.
Age 6 to 12 years

Grandpa tries to answer a tricky question.
Age 6 to 12 years

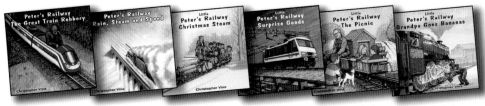

The children foil a plot and cause destruction!
Age 6 to 12 years

A storm, getting wet and stealing a train!
Age 6 to 12 years

Peter saves Christmas, a gentle tale.

A bed-time story with a twist...

A railway picnic soon turns into mayhem...

Playing trains on an epic scale!

Little Peter's Railway - Four gentle tales for younger readers, age 3 to 6 years